This Little Tiger book belongs to:

_____

_____

_____

LITTLE TIGER PRESS LTD,
an imprint of the Little Tiger Group
1 Coda Studios, 189 Munster Road, London SW6 6AW
www.littletiger.co.uk

First published in Great Britain 2020
This edition published 2021

Text and illustrations copyright © Jane Chapman 2020
Visit Jane Chapman at www.ChapmanandWarnes.com
Jane Chapman has asserted her right to be identified as the author and illustrator
of this work under the Copyright, Designs and Patents Act, 1988

A CIP catalogue record for this book is available from the British Library

Printed in China • LTP/1400/2939/0919

1 2 3 4 5 6 7 8 9 10

I Love You With all my Heart

Jane Chapman

LITTLE TiGER

LONDON

Little Bear was playing the drums.
"Look at me!" she shouted.

Ba ba boom! BASH! BANG!

"Wow!" laughed Mummy.
"What a bouncy beat!"

The drumming went
on and on . . .

faster and faster . . .

and louder and louder . . .

until—

CRASH!

—Mummy's favourite plant
was in pieces!

"Oh no!" gasped Little Bear, staring at the mess.
"Mummy will be so cross!"

"I'm sorry, Mummy!"
Little Bear sniffed.
"Oh, sweetheart – never mind,"
smiled Mummy kindly.
"But it was your favourite!"
sobbed her cub.
"And now you'll be sad . . .
and angry . . .
and you won't
love me
any more!"

Mummy pulled Little Bear close.
"I'll ALWAYS love you," she said.
"Put your paw on my heart and
you'll feel my love beating on
and on for ever."
So Little Bear did.

Ba ba boom.

Ba ba boom.

"It beats in your heart too,"
Mummy whispered.
"Can you feel it?"

"I can!
Just like a drum!"
giggled Little Bear.

"Remember,"
said Mummy with a kiss,
"my love will always
be with you, wherever
you are."

Mummy was right. Her love was there
at preschool the very next day.

"I'm going to win!" whooped Little Bear,
racing her friends to the finish line.

But when Badger
overtook her with a

"Wheee!",

Little Bear's feet just
couldn't keep up.

Her breath began
to hurt in her chest
until—

Whump!

—she flopped down on the grass.
"I want Mummy!" Little Bear snuffled.

But Little Bear remembered what Mummy had told her. She put a paw on her chest and—

Ba ba boom
Ba ba boom

—Mummy's love was right there in her heart!

She wiped away her tears and started to smile. "I'm proud of you for trying so hard," said her teacher. "Let's have a snack while we wait for Mummy."

Later, back in the garden,
Little Bear was excited to fly her new kite.
"Yippee!" she cheered, rushing
into the wind.

But a strong gust tugged the string
right out of her paw.

"Come back!" she cried as
the kite sailed away.

"My kite is lost!" thought Little Bear sadly.
But she placed a paw on her heart
to feel Mummy's love.
"I will find that kite," Little Bear decided,
and she marched down the lawn after it.

Dangling from the tree
at the bottom of the garden
was a tail!

"My kite!" laughed Little Bear.
She rushed to grab it . . .

. . . but slipped—

Splash!

—straight into a puddle.

Little Bear shook
the mud from her fur.
"Puddles won't stop me!"
she declared and began to
climb the tree.

Up went Little Bear,
higher and
higher.

"I can do this!"
she mumbled,
her heart beating fast.
Then, holding on tight,
Little Bear reached out as
far as she could . . .

"Got it!"

Little Bear couldn't wait to tell Mummy, so she raced back up the garden to find her.

"I climbed the tree and rescued the kite all by myself!" she sang, dancing round and round . . .

. . . and leaving muddy pawprints
EVERYWHERE!
"Oh, Little Bear! What a mess!"
cried Mummy.
"Outside with all that
mud, please!"

Little Bear put her head in her paws.
"It's all gone wrong!" she sobbed. "I broke the flower,
and lost the race, and now I've made
you dirty . . . and cross!"

Mummy scooped Little Bear into a cuddle.

"Sweetheart, there were good things, too,
like playing the drums and saving your kite!"
she whispered. "And even when I'm cross,
I still love you with all my heart. Can you
hear it beating now?"
And Little Bear could!

Ba ba boom.

Ba ba boom.

"I've made you a surprise,"
beamed Mummy.
"Are you ready?"
She reached into the oven but . . .

"Oh no!" she sighed sadly.
"Your lovely cake is burnt!"
Little Bear took Mummy's paw
and led her outside.

"Even when things go wrong,
I still love you," laughed Little Bear.
"Put your paw on my heart and you'll see."
"Wow!" said Mummy with a smile.
"It's FULL of love! Just like mine!"

More Jane Chapman books you're sure to love . . .

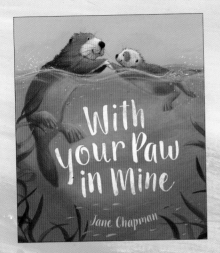

With your Paw in Mine

Jane Chapman

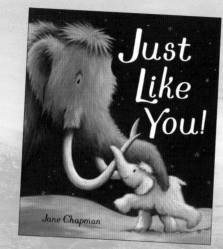

Just Like You!

Jane Chapman

SQUISH SQUASH SQUEEZE!

Pop-up, pull-out ending!

Tracey Corderoy
Jane Chapman

Jane Chapman

Love Enough for Two

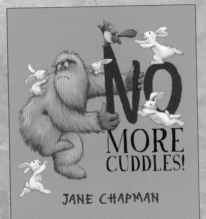

NO MORE CUDDLES!

JANE CHAPMAN

The Little WHITE OWL

Tracey Corderoy   Jane Chapman

For information regarding any of the above titles
or for our catalogue, please contact us:
Little Tiger Press Ltd, 1 Coda Studios,
189 Munster Road, London SW6 6AW
Tel: 020 7385 6333 • E-mail: contact@littletiger.co.uk
www.littletiger.co.uk